Disney · PIXAR
Cars

Look and Find®
WHAT'S DIFFERENT?

Illustrated by Art Mawhinney
Additional illustrations by the Disney Storybook Artists

Published by
Louis Weber, C.E.O., Publications International, Ltd.
7373 North Cicero Avenue, Lincolnwood, Illinois 60712

Ground Floor, 59 Gloucester Place, London W1U 8JJ

Customer Service: 1-800-595-8484 or customer_service@pilbooks.com

www.pilbooks.com

p i kids is a registered trademark of Publications International, Ltd.
Find'em is a trademark of Publications International, Ltd.
Look and Find is a registered trademark of Publications International, Ltd., in the United States and in Canada.

8 7 6 5 4 3 2 1
Manufactured in China.

ISBN-13: 978-1-60553-039-0
ISBN-10: 1-60553-039-5

 publications international, ltd.

Lightning McQueen, Chick Hicks, and The King are in a tight race for the Piston Cup, and the crowd is going wild! Check out the stands to find these things the fans are using to cheer on the race cars.

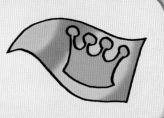

The King knows that success is all about teamwork! He depends on his crew, his fans, and on Mrs. The King, of course! Search this scene to find The King and his biggest supporters.

The King

Luke Pettlework

This Dinocutie

Mrs. The King

The King's crew chief

This fan

Polly Puddlejumper

Doc challenges Lightning to a race on a dirt track. But Lightning is about to discover that the desert is not like the tracks he's used to. He'll want to steer clear of these cactus plants!

Lightning finished fixing the road in Radiator Springs, and it looks good! All the storekeepers in town decide their shops could use some fixing up, too. Look for these things that Luigi and Guido are using to spruce up Luigi's Casa Della Tires.

Squeegee

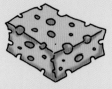

This giant sponge

This can of paint

This scrub brush

Bucket of suds

Broom and dustpan

This paint roller

Woo-hoo! Mater always has fun tractor-tipping, even when Frank chases after him! Hunt around the field to find these things that Mater dropped in his hurry to get away.

This spare tire

An oil can

A crowbar

 A tire iron

 A spare hook

 A roll of duct tape

 A gas can

Lightning and his friends surprise Sally by repairing all the neon lights. Everyone in Radiator Springs is happy to see it return to its old glory! While the cars cruise the strip, search the signs for these lit-up letters.

When reporters get a tip that the missing Lightning McQueen has been spotted in Radiator Springs, they all come looking for the racing star. Scout the crowd to find these Lightning fans.

To break the tie for the Piston Cup, Lightning races once more against Chick Hicks and The King. But this time, Lightning has a new pit crew! Mater brought his collection of lucky charms. Look around the infield to find them all.

Lucky oil can

Lucky orange cone

Lucky map

 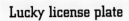 **MATER**

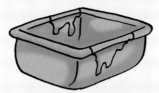

Lucky license plate

Lucky oil pan

Lucky bumper sticker

Lucky spare tire

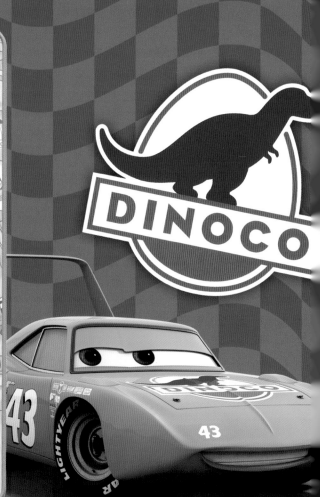

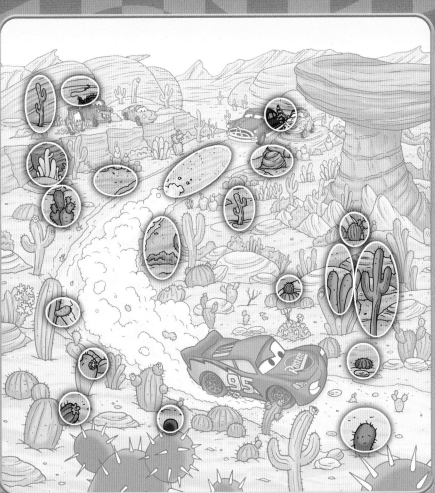

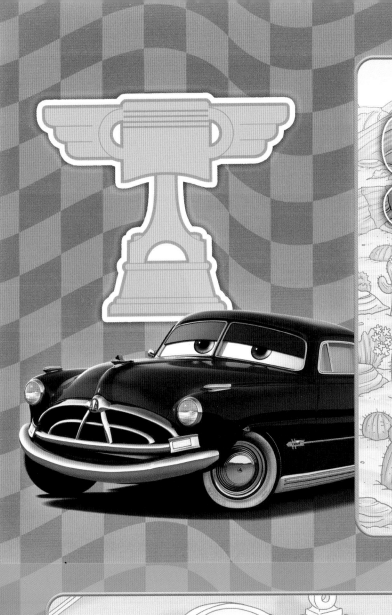

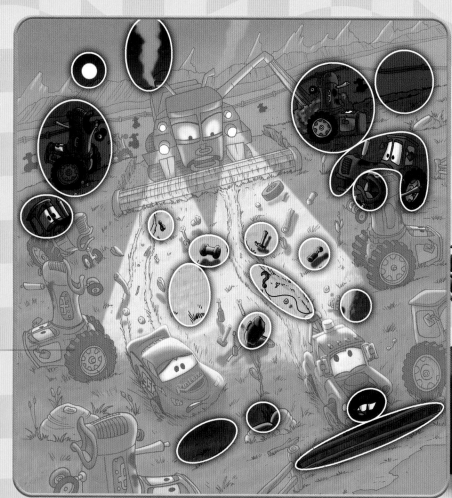